This Walker book belongs to:

_____

_____

_____

For Bill and Yvette
With love and thanks
for all your support

WALKER BOOKS
AND SUBSIDIARIES
LONDON · BOSTON · SYDNEY · AUCKLAND

First published 2019 by Walker Books Ltd, 87 Vauxhall Walk, London SE11 5HJ · This edition published 2020 · © 2019 Sophie Ambrose · The right of Sophie Ambrose to be identified as author/illustrator of this work has been asserted by her in accordance with the Copyright, Designs and Patents Act 1988 · This book has been typeset in Archer · Printed in China · All rights reserved. No part of this book may be reproduced, transmitted or stored in an information retrieval system in any form or by any means, graphic, electronic or mechanical, including photocopying, taping and recording, without prior written permission from the publisher · British Library Cataloguing in Publication Data: a catalogue record for this book is available from the British Library · ISBN 978-1-4063-9288-3 · www.walker.co.uk · 10 9 8 7 6 5 4 3 2 1

Bedtime for Albie

SOPHIE AMBROSE

There was a rosy pink glow in the sky
as the sun was sinking down low.
All the animals knew it was time for bed.
Everyone except for ...

Albie.

"Come on, Albie. It's bedtime now," said Mummy.

"Bedtime?" asked Albie. "Not now!
It's time for rolling and jumping,
sniffling and snuffling. Not bedtime!"
And before Mummy could do anything to stop him,
Albie dashed off!

Skippety trot trit trot.

He went all the way through
the long swishy grass until...

"Hi, Cheetahs!" said Albie.

"Fancy a running race?"

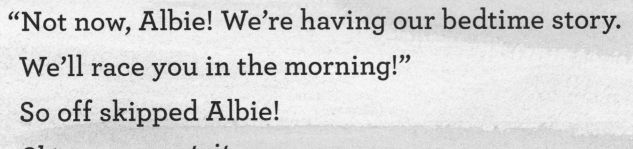

"Not now, Albie! We're having our bedtime story.
We'll race you in the morning!"
So off skipped Albie!
Skippety trot trit trot.

He whooshed right into the clear blue pool of water.

"Hi, Elephants!" said Albie.

"Want to play Splish and Splash?"

"Not now, Albie! We're having our bedtime shower.
We'll play Splish and Splash in the morning!"

So off ran Albie!

Until he came to the deep down burrow.

"Hi, Meercats!" said Albie.

"Let's play who can dig the deepest hole!"

"Not now, Albie!
We're very sleepy.
We'll dig holes with you
in the morning!"
So off snuffled Albie.
Skippety trot trit trot.

"I don't want to go to bed yet," said Albie.

"I want to roll and jump and sniffle and snuffle!

If nobody will play with me, I'll just play by myself."

And off he went! *Skippety trot trit trot.*

But it was dusk and it really was getting dark now.
Albie could hear mysterious noises all around him.

The rustlings and scratchings of the night.

Hissss!

"Who's there?" asked Albie in a small voice.

"Hi, Albie," said Snake. "It's just me!"

Albie trotted on a little further.

He saw a pair of big eyes glinting at him in the bushes!

Toowit Toowoo! "W-what's that?" stuttered Albie.

"Hi, Albie," said Owl. "It's just me! Shouldn't you be in bed?"

The stars were twinkling in the warm night sky.
"I don't want to play by myself any more,"
Albie said sleepily. "I just want my mummy."

He snuffled and sniffled –

and came across a familiar,
wet, muddy smell.

Then he snuffled and sniffled
some more until...

"Hi, Albie!" said the Hippos.

"Let's get you home!"

Mummy and Albie snuggled up tight.

"I'm ready for bed now," said Albie.

"Thank goodness," said Mummy.

"But before you go to bed ...

it's time for your mud bath!"

Albie rolled and jumped and splished and splashed!

It was the best game he had played all day.

In fact, it was so much fun ...

that all of Albie's friends wanted to join in too!
They had the gloopiest, splashiest, noisiest
mud bath party under the stars ever!

Until ...

it really was bedtime for Albie.

"Night night, Albie."